HENRY
AND THE
VALENTINE SURPRISE

NANCY CARLSON

VIKING

TO BARRY,

I AM GLAD WE BUMPED HEADS
34 YEARS AGO AT THE YMCA!

MUCH LOVE,
NANCY

VIKING
Published by Penguin Group
Penguin Young Readers Group, 345 Hudson Street, New York, New York 10014, U.S.A.
Penguin Group (Canada), 90 Eglinton Avenue East, Suite 700, Toronto, Ontario, Canada M4P 2Y3
(a division of Pearson Penguin Canada Inc.)
Penguin Books Ltd, 80 Strand, London WC2R 0RL, England
Penguin Ireland, 25 St Stephen's Green, Dublin 2, Ireland (a division of Penguin Books Ltd)
Penguin Group (Australia), 250 Camberwell Road, Camberwell, Victoria 3124, Australia
(a division of Pearson Australia Group Pty Ltd)
Penguin Books India Pvt Ltd, 11 Community Centre, Panchsheel Park, New Delhi – 110 017, India
Penguin Group (NZ), 67 Apollo Drive, Rosedale, North Shore 0632, New Zealand
(a division of Pearson New Zealand Ltd)
Penguin Books (South Africa) (Pty) Ltd, 24 Sturdee Avenue, Rosebank, Johannesburg 2196, South Africa

First published in 2008 by Viking, a division of Penguin Young Readers Group

1 3 5 7 9 10 8 6 4 2

Copyright © Nancy Carlson, 2008

LIBRARY OF CONGRESS CATALOGING-IN-PUBLICATION DATA
Carlson, Nancy L.
Henry and the Valentine surprise / Nancy Carlson.
p. cm.
Summary: When Henry and his first-grade classmates notice a heart-shaped box on their
teacher's desk the day before Valentine's Day, they try to find out if he has a girlfriend.
ISBN 978-0-670-06267-6 (hardcover)
[1. Valentine's Day—Fiction. 2. Teachers—Fiction. 3. Schools—Fiction.] I. Title.
PZ7.C21665Hcm 2008
[E]—dc22
2008001283

Manufactured in China
Set in Avenir

Tomorrow was Valentine's Day, and Henry and his classmates found a heart-shaped box on Mr. McCarthy's desk.

"I wonder if Mr. McCarthy has a girlfriend," said Sydney.

"Teachers don't have girlfriends. They never leave school," said Henry.

"That's not true!" said Tony. "I once saw Mr. McCarthy at the grocery store!"

"Let's find out if Mr. McCarthy has a girlfriend," said Henry.

So during recess, they spied on Mr. McCarthy

talking to Ms. Olson, the playground monitor.

At lunch, they saw the lunch lady

give Mr. McCarthy an extra tuna melt.

Later, Tony spied on Mr. McCarthy

eating lunch with the French teacher!

"Wow! Mr. McCarthy has a lot of girlfriends," said Henry.

At the end of the day, Henry asked,
"Who is that valentine for?"

"I will tell you tomorrow at the party," said Mr. McCarthy. "Now it's time to go home and work on valentines for all of your classmates."

"Even girls?" asked Henry.
"Yes," said Mr. McCarthy. "Please make
a valentine for everyone in the class."

After school, Henry made valentines for everyone in his class, including the girls.

Henry even put an extra candy heart in Sydney's valentine.

The next day, everyone was excited about the party,

and Mr. McCarthy was looking sharp.

When it was time for the party, Henry asked again, "Who is that valentine for?"

"Well, this very special valentine is for . . .

". . . all of you!"

"Is that fish food?" asked Sydney.
"And that's a net!" said Tony.
"But we're not fish!" said Henry.

"No, but your new class pets are!"
"Yay!" cheered the class.

"There are twenty fish. One for everyone in the class to name. You can even make a special valentine for the fish you name!"

"Yippie!"

"See, I told you teachers don't have girlfriends," said Henry.

"Yeah," said Tony. "Teachers are too busy . . .

". . . teaching!"